Nibble, Nosh and Gnasher

Written and illustrated
by Shoo Rayner

Collins

In the furthest, most-deserted sector of space, a colossal ball of garbage floated in the darkness.

Everything horrible that you could ever imagine was glued together with piles of toxic, slimy goo!

The Galaxy Express was running late, so it took a shortcut. Squish! Squash! Splat! The spaceship piled into the massive gloopy wreck of rubbish.

"The steering wheel is stuck!" cried the commander of the Galaxy Express.

Not far away, the Clean Team were hard at work.
Nosh, Gnasher and Nibble were crunching scraps of old
rockets and burnt-out shooting stars that had fallen on
Knick-Knack, the little planet they called home.

Nibble got an urgent message. "It's an emergency," she told Nosh and Gnasher.

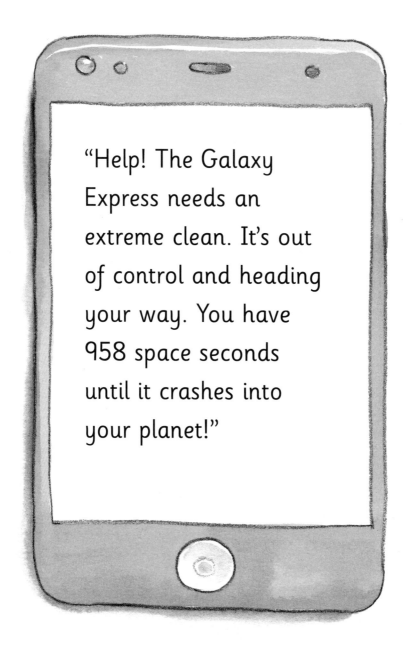

"Help! The Galaxy Express needs an extreme clean. It's out of control and heading your way. You have 958 space seconds until it crashes into your planet!"

"Quick! Call a space taxi," Nibble cried. "We have to stop this catastrophe!"

"Take us to the Galaxy Express," Nibble told the taxi driver.
"Hurry up!"

The taxi hurtled off like a frenzied meteor.

The alien taxi driver was gigantic, with eight tentacles.
The Clean Team had never seen an alien like him.

"What a huge mouth he has!" Gnasher whispered to his friends, as they landed on the wretched spaceship.

"He looks terrifying!" said Nosh.

10

"Get to work!" Nibble ordered. "We now have 800 space seconds to prevent this catastrophe!"

The taxi driver licked his dribbling lips and smiled a slimy, hungry smile as he watched the Clean Team work.

The space seconds ticked by. The Clean Team gobbled up empty tins and cardboard boxes ... old spacesuits, pants and socks ... cracked and broken phones and laptops ... crumpled wrapping paper and gnarly garden gnomes.

"Yuck!" called the taxi driver. "How can you eat that crunchy garbage?"

Time was running out. Planet Knick-Knack was getting closer and larger by the second. The Galaxy Express was still covered in slimy, toxic goo!

"Disgusting!" said Nibble. "We can't eat that!"

"60 space seconds to impact!" yelled Gnasher.

"We're going to crash and die!" wailed Nosh.

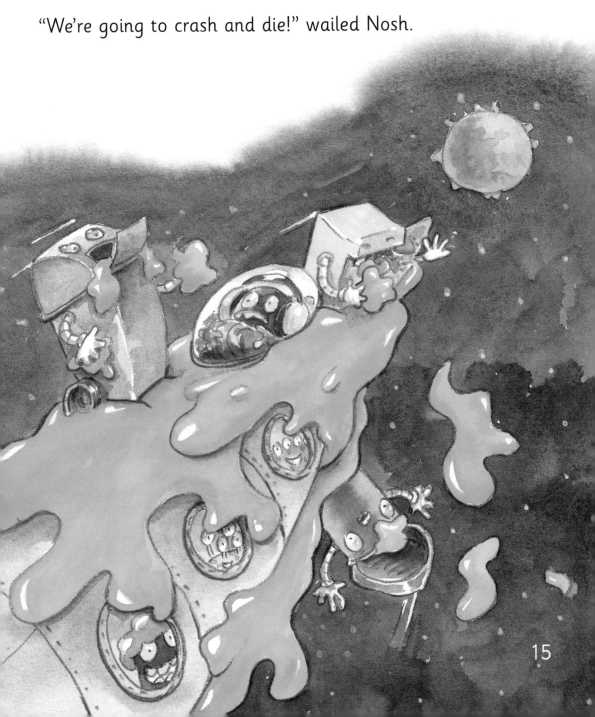

"Stand back!" the taxi driver roared.

"Toxic goo is delicious!"

In one gigantic wriggling lick, the taxi driver slurped up all the sticky, icky goo.

Now the Galaxy Express was gunk-free and squeaky-clean,
the commander could steer the spaceship again.
"Phew!" he cried.

The Galaxy Express swerved past Planet Knick-Knack and disappeared into space. But Nibble, Nosh and Gnasher had gone too! The Clean Team had disappeared into thin air!

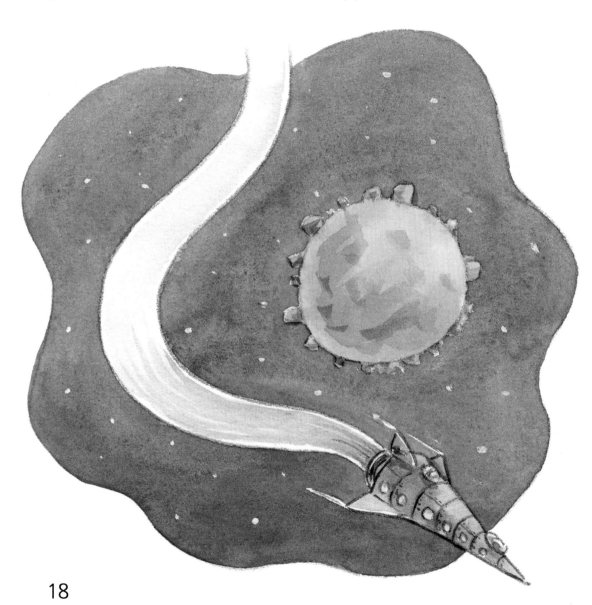

The taxi driver smiled and smacked his lips.

Then his stomach began to rumble. It grumbled, boomed and groaned into a whopping, great, colossal noise!

Squish! Squash! Splat! Nibble, Nosh and Gnasher popped out of the driver's mouth and landed in the back seat of his taxi!

"Good job!" the taxi driver chortled. "Maybe I should join your team?"

"Maybe," Nibble said, trembling. "J-just d-don't call us. W-we'll call you!"

Can you:

- **Gobble up space rubbish?**
- **Stop disasters?**
- **Save Planet Knick-Knack?**

Join the Clean Team!

 After reading

Letters and Sounds: Phases 5-6

Word count: 495

Focus phonemes: /n/ kn gn /r/ wr /s/ c /c/ x, /sh/ ci, /m/ mb

Common exception words: of, to, the, into, so, said, were, one, friend, great

Curriculum links: PSHE

National Curriculum learning objectives: Spoken language: listen and respond appropriately to adults and their peers; Reading/Word reading: apply phonic knowledge and skills as the route to decode words, read accurately by blending sounds in unfamiliar words containing GPCs that have been taught, read common exception words, read other words of more than one syllable that contain taught GPCs, read aloud accurately books that are consistent with their developing phonic knowledge; Reading/Comprehension: understand both the books that they can already read accurately and fluently ... by making inferences on the basis of what is being said and done

Developing fluency

- Your child may enjoy hearing you read the story. Model reading dialogue with expression.
- Now ask your child to read some of the dialogue with lots of expression to portray the urgency of the story.

Phonic practice

- Help your child to practise reading words with suffixes. Ask your child to read each of these words, firstly without and then with the suffix added:

  gloop gloopy   crunch crunchy   squeak squeaky   slime slimy

- Can your child tell you how the suffix changes the root word? (*it changes a noun into an adjective*)
- Talk about the last example (slime) and how with some words the spelling of the root word changes when you add a suffix. In this example, you delete the 'e' when you add the 'y' slime - slimy.
- Model sounding out the word 'wretched' (wr/e/tch/ed), drawing attention to the spelling of the /r/ phoneme (wr).
  - Now ask your child to sound out 'wretched' and blend the sounds together.
  - Look at page 16. Ask your child to find two words that start with the /r/ phoneme. (*roared, wrigging*)
  - Discuss the different ways of writing the /r/ phoneme. (wr, r)